The

Journal

Bonni Goldberg
Vizye Publications
Portland, OR

Published by Vizye Publications in 2017
First edition; First printing

Design and writing © 2017 Bonni Goldberg
Cover by Kayla Himmelberger

ISBN: 978-09967-524-2-8

Dedication

This journal is dedicated to
all those who love to taste,
sample & size up the
abundance of food & drink
whenever & wherever
the opportunity presents!

Introduction

What was that delicious wine, that perfect olive oil, that fabulous cheese, that just right pear variety, that tea your sister loved, the third beer in the flight you ordered, the salsa they were sampling at the market last week? Never forget again!

I created this journal because I know you're out there: others like me who love to try new foods and drinks, who get pleasure from experiencing the differences in varieties of the same item, who get excited by the trays and plates of samples laid out in your favorite food and beverage stores.

These days, shopping can be a gourmet experience. But with all the opportunities to try new foods and flavors, it's hard to keep track of what you like, why you like it, and when you want to bring it home.

How many times have you sampled something and thought to yourself, this would be perfect for _____ (fill-in-the-blank: a summer brunch, to bring to the next potluck, to serve when a certain friend comes over, to add to fruit pies, etc.), only to either forget what it was, or where you found it, or –if you bought it– when you wanted to use it.

The Tasting Journal is ideal to keep track of tasting adventures if you love to sample and taste wherever you go. Keep a record of your favorites in this perfect traveling companion and be able to find whatever you've sampled and loved whenever you want it.

Compile your personal tasting notes with space to write down the specific elements you liked and your ideas of when to serve it.

With a fill-in table of contents, turn right to the page you need. If there are specific categories you always return to, like red wines or holiday dinners, use the table of content to create these sections too.

With this journal, go forth and keep track of every unusual, delicious, and memorable item that you discover at specialty shops, festivals, farmers markets, tasting events, and free samples everywhere.

Table of Contents

Table of Contents

Table of Contents

Table of Contents

Table of Contents

Table of Contents

As we say in the American
Institute of Wine and Food....
A little bit of everything....
And have a good time.
—Julia Child

Taste as you go.
—Anne Burrell

If I'm a lush at anything,
it's food and drink.
—Hugh Jackman

Item: _____

Price: _____

Location: _____

Rating: 😙 😙 😙 😙 😙

What I like best about it:

_____

_____

_____

_____

_____

Ideas for where & when:

_____

_____

_____

_____

_____

Item:_____

Price:_____

Location:_____

Rating: 👄 👄 👄 👄 👄

What I like best about it:

_____

_____

_____

_____

_____

Ideas for where & when:

_____

_____

_____

_____

_____

Item: _____

Price: _____

Location: _____

Rating: 😚 😚 😚 😚 😚

What I like best about it:

_____

_____

_____

_____

_____

Ideas for where & when:

_____

_____

_____

_____

_____

Item: _____

Price: _____

Location: _____

Rating: 👄 👄 👄 👄 👄

What I like best about it:

_____

_____

_____

_____

_____

Ideas for where & when:

_____

_____

_____

_____

_____

Item:_____

Price:_____

Location: _____

Rating: 👄 👄 👄 👄 👄

What I like best about it:

_____

_____

_____

_____

_____

Ideas for where & when:

_____

_____

_____

_____

_____

Item:_____

Price:_____

Location:_____

Rating: 👄 👄 👄 👄 👄

What I like best about it:

_____

_____

_____

_____

_____

Ideas for where & when:

_____

_____

_____

_____

_____

Item: _____

Price: _____

Location: _____

Rating: 👄 👄 👄 👄 👄

What I like best about it:

_____

_____

_____

_____

_____

Ideas for where & when:

_____

_____

_____

_____

_____

Item:_____

Price:_____

Location:_____

Rating: 😋 😋 😋 😋 😋

What I like best about it:

_____

_____

_____

_____

_____

Ideas for where & when:

_____

_____

_____

_____

_____

Item: _____

Price: _____

Location: _____

Rating: 👄 👄 👄 👄 👄

What I like best about it:

_____

_____

_____

_____

_____

Ideas for where & when:

_____

_____

_____

_____

_____

Item:_____

Price:_____

Location:_____

Rating: 😚 😚 😚 😚 😚

What I like best about it:

_____

_____

_____

_____

_____

Ideas for where & when:

_____

_____

_____

_____

_____

Item:_____

Price:_____

Location:_____

Rating: 👄 👄 👄 👄 👄

What I like best about it:

_____

_____

_____

_____

_____

Ideas for where & when:

_____

_____

_____

_____

_____

Item:_____

Price:_____

Location:_____

Rating: 👄 👄 👄 👄 👄

What I like best about it:

_____

_____

_____

_____

_____

Ideas for where & when:

_____

_____

_____

_____

_____

Item: _____

Price: _____

Location: _____

Rating: 👄 👄 👄 👄 👄

What I like best about it:

_____

_____

_____

_____

_____

Ideas for where & when:

_____

_____

_____

_____

_____

Item:_____

Price:_____

Location:_____

Rating: 👄 👄 👄 👄 👄

What I like best about it:

_____

_____

_____

_____

_____

Ideas for where & when:

_____

_____

_____

_____

_____

Item:_____

Price:_____

Location:_____

Rating: 😋 😋 😋 😋 😋

What I like best about it:

_____

_____

_____

_____

_____

Ideas for where & when:

_____

_____

_____

_____

_____

Item:_____

Price:_____

Location:_____

Rating: 👄 👄 👄 👄 👄

What I like best about it:

_____

_____

_____

_____

_____

Ideas for where & when:

_____

_____

_____

_____

_____

Item: _____

Price: _____

Location: _____

Rating: 👄 👄 👄 👄 👄

What I like best about it:

_____

_____

_____

_____

_____

Ideas for where & when:

_____

_____

_____

_____

_____

Item:_____

Price:_____

Location:_____

Rating: 👄 👄 👄 👄 👄

What I like best about it:

_____

_____

_____

_____

_____

Ideas for where & when:

_____

_____

_____

_____

_____

Item:_____

Price:_____

Location:_____

Rating: 👄 👄 👄 👄 👄

What I like best about it:

_____

_____

_____

_____

_____

Ideas for where & when:

_____

_____

_____

_____

_____

Item: _____

Price: _____

Location: _____

Rating: 👄 👄 👄 👄 👄

What I like best about it:

_____

_____

_____

_____

_____

Ideas for where & when:

_____

_____

_____

_____

_____

Item: _____

Price: _____

Location: _____

Rating: 😄 😄 😄 😄 😄

What I like best about it:

_____

_____

_____

_____

_____

Ideas for where & when:

_____

_____

_____

_____

_____

Item: _____

Price: _____

Location: _____

Rating: 😗 😗 😗 😗 😗

What I like best about it:

_____

_____

_____

_____

_____

Ideas for where & when:

_____

_____

_____

_____

_____

Item: _____

Price: _____

Location: _____

Rating: 👄 👄 👄 👄 👄

What I like best about it:

_____

_____

_____

_____

_____

Ideas for where & when:

_____

_____

_____

_____

_____

Item: _____

Price: _____

Location: _____

Rating: 😙 😙 😙 😙 😙

What I like best about it:

_____

_____

_____

_____

_____

Ideas for where & when:

_____

_____

_____

_____

_____

Item:_____

Price:_____

Location:_____

Rating: 👄 👄 👄 👄 👄

What I like best about it:

_____

_____

_____

_____

_____

Ideas for where & when:

_____

_____

_____

_____

_____

Item: _____

Price: _____

Location: _____

Rating: 👄 👄 👄 👄 👄

What I like best about it:

_____

_____

_____

_____

_____

Ideas for where & when:

_____

_____

_____

_____

_____

Item: _____

Price: _____

Location: _____

Rating: 👄 👄 👄 👄 👄

What I like best about it:

_____

_____

_____

_____

_____

Ideas for where & when:

_____

_____

_____

_____

_____

Item:_____

Price:_____

Location:_____

Rating: 👄 👄 👄 👄 👄

What I like best about it:

_____

_____

_____

_____

_____

Ideas for where & when:

_____

_____

_____

_____

_____

Item:_____

Price:_____

Location:_____

Rating: 😋 😋 😋 😋 😋

What I like best about it:

_____

_____

_____

_____

_____

Ideas for where & when:

_____

_____

_____

_____

_____

Item:_____

Price:_____

Location:_____

Rating: 👄 👄 👄 👄 👄

What I like best about it:

_____

_____

_____

_____

_____

Ideas for where & when:

_____

_____

_____

_____

_____

Item:_____

Price:_____

Location:_____

Rating: 😙 😙 😙 😙 😙

What I like best about it:

_____

_____

_____

_____

_____

Ideas for where & when:

_____

_____

_____

_____

_____

Item:_____

Price:_____

Location:_____

Rating: 😛 😛 😛 😛 😛

What I like best about it:

_____

_____

_____

_____

_____

Ideas for where & when:

_____

_____

_____

_____

_____

Item:_____

Price:_____

Location:_____

Rating: 👄 👄 👄 👄 👄

What I like best about it:

_____

_____

_____

_____

_____

Ideas for where & when:

_____

_____

_____

_____

_____

Item:_____

Price:_____

Location:_____

Rating: 👄 👄 👄 👄 👄

What I like best about it:

_____

_____

_____

_____

_____

Ideas for where & when:

_____

_____

_____

_____

_____

Item:_____

Price:_____

Location:_____

Rating: 👄 👄 👄 👄 👄

What I like best about it:

_____

_____

_____

_____

_____

Ideas for where & when:

_____

_____

_____

_____

_____

Item:_____

Price:_____

Location:_____

Rating: 👄 👄 👄 👄 👄

What I like best about it:

_____

_____

_____

_____

_____

Ideas for where & when:

_____

_____

_____

_____

_____

Item: _____

Price: _____

Location: _____

Rating: 👄 👄 👄 👄 👄

What I like best about it:

_____

_____

_____

_____

_____

Ideas for where & when:

_____

_____

_____

_____

_____

Item:_____

Price:_____

Location:_____

Rating: 👄 👄 👄 👄 👄

What I like best about it:

_____

_____

_____

_____

_____

Ideas for where & when:

_____

_____

_____

_____

_____

Item:_____

Price:_____

Location:_____

Rating: 😋 😋 😋 😋 😋

What I like best about it:

_____

_____

_____

_____

_____

Ideas for where & when:

_____

_____

_____

_____

_____

Item: _____

Price: _____

Location: _____

Rating: 👄 👄 👄 👄 👄

What I like best about it:

_____

_____

_____

_____

_____

Ideas for where & when:

_____

_____

_____

_____

_____

Item:_____

Price:_____

Location:_____

Rating: 👄 👄 👄 👄 👄

What I like best about it:

_____

_____

_____

_____

_____

Ideas for where & when:

_____

_____

_____

_____

_____

Item:_____

Price:_____

Location:_____

Rating: 👄 👄 👄 👄 👄

What I like best about it:

_____
_____
_____
_____
_____

Ideas for where & when:

_____
_____
_____
_____
_____

Item:_____

Price:_____

Location:_____

Rating: 👄 👄 👄 👄 👄

What I like best about it:

_____

_____

_____

_____

_____

Ideas for where & when:

_____

_____

_____

_____

_____

Item:_____

Price:_____

Location:_____

Rating: 👄 👄 👄 👄 👄

What I like best about it:

_____

_____

_____

_____

_____

Ideas for where & when:

_____

_____

_____

_____

_____

Item: _____

Price: _____

Location: _____

Rating: 👄 👄 👄 👄 👄

What I like best about it:

_____

_____

_____

_____

_____

Ideas for where & when:

_____

_____

_____

_____

_____

Item:_____

Price:_____

Location:_____

Rating: 👄 👄 👄 👄 👄

What I like best about it:

_____

_____

_____

_____

_____

Ideas for where & when:

_____

_____

_____

_____

_____

Item:_____

Price:_____

Location:_____

Rating: 😊 😊 😊 😊 😊

What I like best about it:

_____

_____

_____

_____

_____

Ideas for where & when:

_____

_____

_____

_____

_____

Item:_____

Price:_____

Location:_____

Rating: 👄 👄 👄 👄 👄

What I like best about it:

_____

_____

_____

_____

_____

Ideas for where & when:

_____

_____

_____

_____

_____

Item:_____

Price:_____

Location:_____

Rating: 😊 😊 😊 😊 😊

What I like best about it:

_____

_____

_____

_____

_____

Ideas for where & when:

_____

_____

_____

_____

_____

Item:_____

Price:_____

Location:_____

Rating: 👄 👄 👄 👄 👄

What I like best about it:

_____

_____

_____

_____

_____

Ideas for where & when:

_____

_____

_____

_____

_____

Item: _____

Price: _____

Location: _____

Rating: 👄 👄 👄 👄 👄

What I like best about it:

_____

_____

_____

_____

_____

Ideas for where & when:

_____

_____

_____

_____

_____

Item:_____

Price:_____

Location:_____

Rating: 👄 👄 👄 👄 👄

What I like best about it:

_____

_____

_____

_____

_____

Ideas for where & when:

_____

_____

_____

_____

_____

Item: _____

Price: _____

Location: _____

Rating: 😚 😚 😚 😚 😚

What I like best about it:

_____

_____

_____

_____

_____

Ideas for where & when:

_____

_____

_____

_____

_____

Item: _____

Price: _____

Location: _____

Rating: 😙 😙 😙 😙 😙

What I like best about it:

_____

_____

_____

_____

_____

Ideas for where & when:

_____

_____

_____

_____

_____

Item: _____

Price: _____

Location: _____

Rating: 👄 👄 👄 👄 👄

What I like best about it:

_____

_____

_____

_____

_____

Ideas for where & when:

_____

_____

_____

_____

_____

Item:_____

Price:_____

Location:_____

Rating: 👄 👄 👄 👄 👄

What I like best about it:

_____

_____

_____

_____

_____

Ideas for where & when:

_____

_____

_____

_____

_____

Item: _____

Price: _____

Location: _____

Rating: 😙 😙 😙 😙 😙

What I like best about it:

_____

_____

_____

_____

_____

Ideas for where & when:

_____

_____

_____

_____

_____

Item:_____

Price:_____

Location:_____

Rating: 👄 👄 👄 👄 👄

What I like best about it:

_____

_____

_____

_____

_____

Ideas for where & when:

_____

_____

_____

_____

_____

Item:_____

Price:_____

Location:_____

Rating: 👄 👄 👄 👄 👄

What I like best about it:

_____

_____

_____

_____

_____

Ideas for where & when:

_____

_____

_____

_____

_____

Item:_____

Price:_____

Location:_____

Rating: 👄 👄 👄 👄 👄

What I like best about it:

_____

_____

_____

_____

_____

Ideas for where & when:

_____

_____

_____

_____

_____

Item:_____

Price:_____

Location:_____

Rating: 😋 😋 😋 😋 😋

What I like best about it:

_____

_____

_____

_____

_____

Ideas for where & when:

_____

_____

_____

_____

_____

Item:_____

Price:_____

Location:_____

Rating: 👄 👄 👄 👄 👄

What I like best about it:

_____

_____

_____

_____

_____

Ideas for where & when:

_____

_____

_____

_____

_____

Item:_____

Price:_____

Location:_____

Rating: 😋 😋 😋 😋 😋

What I like best about it:

_____

_____

_____

_____

_____

Ideas for where & when:

_____

_____

_____

_____

_____

Item:_____

Price:_____

Location:_____

Rating: 👄 👄 👄 👄 👄

What I like best about it:

_____

_____

_____

_____

_____

Ideas for where & when:

_____

_____

_____

_____

_____

Item:_____

Price:_____

Location:_____

Rating: 👄 👄 👄 👄 👄

What I like best about it:

_____

_____

_____

_____

_____

Ideas for where & when:

_____

_____

_____

_____

_____

Item:_____

Price:_____

Location:_____

Rating: 👄 👄 👄 👄 👄

What I like best about it:

_____

_____

_____

_____

_____

Ideas for where & when:

_____

_____

_____

_____

_____

Item:_____

Price:_____

Location:_____

Rating: 👄 👄 👄 👄 👄

What I like best about it:

_____

_____

_____

_____

_____

Ideas for where & when:

_____

_____

_____

_____

_____

Item:_____

Price:_____

Location:_____

Rating: 👄 👄 👄 👄 👄

What I like best about it:

_____

_____

_____

_____

_____

Ideas for where & when:

_____

_____

_____

_____

_____

Item: _____

Price: _____

Location: _____

Rating: 👄 👄 👄 👄 👄

What I like best about it:

_____

_____

_____

_____

_____

Ideas for where & when:

_____

_____

_____

_____

_____

Item: _____

Price: _____

Location: _____

Rating: 👄 👄 👄 👄 👄

What I like best about it:

_____

_____

_____

_____

_____

Ideas for where & when:

_____

_____

_____

_____

_____

Item:_____

Price:_____

Location:_____

Rating: 👄 👄 👄 👄 👄

What I like best about it:

_____

_____

_____

_____

_____

Ideas for where & when:

_____

_____

_____

_____

_____

Item:_____

Price:_____

Location:_____

Rating: 👄 👄 👄 👄 👄

What I like best about it:

_____

_____

_____

_____

_____

Ideas for where & when:

_____

_____

_____

_____

_____

Item: _____

Price: _____

Location: _____

Rating: 😊 😊 😊 😊 😊

What I like best about it:

_____

_____

_____

_____

_____

Ideas for where & when:

_____

_____

_____

_____

_____

Item:_____

Price:_____

Location:_____

Rating: 😋 😋 😋 😋 😋

What I like best about it:

_____

_____

_____

_____

_____

Ideas for where & when:

_____

_____

_____

_____

_____

Item: _____

Price: _____

Location: _____

Rating: 👄 👄 👄 👄 👄

What I like best about it:

_____

_____

_____

_____

_____

Ideas for where & when:

_____

_____

_____

_____

_____

Item:_____

Price:_____

Location:_____

Rating: 👄 👄 👄 👄 👄

What I like best about it:

_____

_____

_____

_____

_____

Ideas for where & when:

_____

_____

_____

_____

_____

Item: _____

Price: _____

Location: _____

Rating: 👄 👄 👄 👄 👄

What I like best about it:

_____
_____
_____
_____
_____

Ideas for where & when:

_____
_____
_____
_____
_____

Item:_____

Price:_____

Location:_____

Rating: 👄 👄 👄 👄 👄

What I like best about it:

_____

_____

_____

_____

_____

Ideas for where & when:

_____

_____

_____

_____

_____

Item: _____

Price: _____

Location: _____

Rating: 😋 😋 😋 😋 😋

What I like best about it:

_____

_____

_____

_____

_____

Ideas for where & when:

_____

_____

_____

_____

_____

Item:_____

Price:_____

Location:_____

Rating: 😋 😋 😋 😋 😋

What I like best about it:

_____

_____

_____

_____

_____

Ideas for where & when:

_____

_____

_____

_____

_____

Item:_____

Price:_____

Location:_____

Rating: 👄 👄 👄 👄 👄

What I like best about it:

_____

_____

_____

_____

_____

Ideas for where & when:

_____

_____

_____

_____

_____

Item:_____

Price:_____

Location:_____

Rating: 👄 👄 👄 👄 👄

What I like best about it:

_____

_____

_____

_____

_____

Ideas for where & when:

_____

_____

_____

_____

_____

Item: _____

Price: _____

Location: _____

Rating: 😚 😚 😚 😚 😚

What I like best about it:

_____

_____

_____

_____

_____

Ideas for where & when:

_____

_____

_____

_____

_____

Item:_____

Price:_____

Location:_____

Rating: 👄 👄 👄 👄 👄

What I like best about it:

_____

_____

_____

_____

_____

Ideas for where & when:

_____

_____

_____

_____

_____

Item: _____

Price: _____

Location: _____

Rating: 😋 😋 😋 😋 😋

What I like best about it:

_____

_____

_____

_____

_____

Ideas for where & when:

_____

_____

_____

_____

_____

Item:_____

Price:_____

Location:_____

Rating: 😋 😋 😋 😋 😋

What I like best about it:

_____

_____

_____

_____

_____

Ideas for where & when:

_____

_____

_____

_____

_____

Item:_____

Price:_____

Location:_____

Rating: 👄 👄 👄 👄 👄

What I like best about it:

_____
_____
_____
_____
_____

Ideas for where & when:

_____
_____
_____
_____
_____

Item:_____

Price:_____

Location:_____

Rating: 👄 👄 👄 👄 👄

What I like best about it:

_____

_____

_____

_____

_____

Ideas for where & when:

_____

_____

_____

_____

_____

Item: _____

Price: _____

Location: _____

Rating: 👄 👄 👄 👄 👄

What I like best about it:

_____

_____

_____

_____

_____

Ideas for where & when:

_____

_____

_____

_____

_____

Item:_____

Price:_____

Location:_____

Rating: 👄 👄 👄 👄 👄

What I like best about it:

_____

_____

_____

_____

_____

Ideas for where & when:

_____

_____

_____

_____

_____

Item: _____

Price: _____

Location: _____

Rating: 👄 👄 👄 👄 👄

What I like best about it:

_____

_____

_____

_____

_____

Ideas for where & when:

_____

_____

_____

_____

_____

Item:_____

Price:_____

Location:_____

Rating: 👄 👄 👄 👄 👄

What I like best about it:

_____

_____

_____

_____

_____

Ideas for where & when:

_____

_____

_____

_____

_____

Item:_____

Price:_____

Location:_____

Rating: 👄 👄 👄 👄 👄

What I like best about it:

_____

_____

_____

_____

_____

Ideas for where & when:

_____

_____

_____

_____

_____

Item:_____

Price:_____

Location:_____

Rating: 👄 👄 👄 👄 👄

What I like best about it:

_____

_____

_____

_____

_____

Ideas for where & when:

_____

_____

_____

_____

_____

Item:_____

Price:_____

Location:_____

Rating: 👄 👄 👄 👄 👄

What I like best about it:

_____

_____

_____

_____

_____

Ideas for where & when:

_____

_____

_____

_____

_____

Item:_____

Price:_____

Location:_____

Rating: 👄 👄 👄 👄 👄

What I like best about it:

_____

_____

_____

_____

_____

Ideas for where & when:

_____

_____

_____

_____

_____

Item: _____

Price: _____

Location: _____

Rating: 👄 👄 👄 👄 👄

What I like best about it:

_____

_____

_____

_____

_____

Ideas for where & when:

_____

_____

_____

_____

_____

Item:_____

Price:_____

Location:_____

Rating: 👄 👄 👄 👄 👄

What I like best about it:

_____

_____

_____

_____

_____

Ideas for where & when:

_____

_____

_____

_____

_____

Item: _____

Price: _____

Location: _____

Rating: 👄 👄 👄 👄 👄

What I like best about it:

_____

_____

_____

_____

_____

Ideas for where & when:

_____

_____

_____

_____

_____

Item:_____

Price:_____

Location:_____

Rating: 👄 👄 👄 👄 👄

What I like best about it:

_____

_____

_____

_____

_____

Ideas for where & when:

_____

_____

_____

_____

_____